DISNEP Junior
MICKEY MOUSE CLUBHOUSE
MINNIE'S PET SALON

Adapted by **Bill Scollon**

Based on the episode written by **Ashley Mendoza**

Illustrated by **Loter, Inc.**

DISNEP PRESS

Los Angeles • New York

Today is the day of Pluto's All-Star Pet Show! All the Clubhouse pets will be on stage. But only one will win the prize for Best in Show!

Minnie will help get the pets ready. "Welcome to Minnie's Pet Salon," she says. "It's time for me to open for business!"

The gang brings their pets to the salon.
Goofy brings his kitty, **Mr. Pettibone**. "And my frog,
Fiona, needs to get ready, too," he says.
Daisy drops off her bunny, **Captain Jumps-a-Lot**.

"Here's my adorable puppy, Bella," says Clarabelle. Pete is right behind her. "I'm dropping off Butch!" he says. Then Donald runs up. "Boo-Boo Chicken wants to come, too!"

The first station is the Dog and Cat Wash.
Daisy and Pluto are ready to give Bella a bath. Daisy fills
the tub with warm water and pours in the bath soap.
Pink bubbles grow and grow!
"Oh, no!" says Daisy. "There are too many bubbles."
She jumps into the tub to find Bella.

Minnie comes to the rescue. "We need a Mouseketool!" she says.

Toodles brings a baby elephant.

She fills her trunk with water and rinses the bubbles away. **"Yay!"** shouts Daisy. "Now Bella is ready for Pluto's pet show."

Over at the Beauty Bar, Donald is trying to put bows on Figaro and Mr. Pettibone, but they won't sit still!

Minnie brings Toodles over to help. Toodles has three Mouseketools left.

"Let's try the beach towel," Minnie says.

Donald holds the beach towel, and Figaro and
Mr. Pettibone jump right in.

"What a **purr-fect** solution," says Minnie. Then she
and Donald put bows on each kitty.

"Thanks for helping me, Minnie," says Donald.

Next Minnie goes to check on Mickey. He's trying to teach
Captain Jumps-a-Lot and Fiona to jump together.
"Maybe they'll do it if we give them a beat," says Minnie.

Mickey and Minnie jump together and chant, "One, two, jump when we do. Three, four, jump once more."
It works! The bunny and frog hop at the same time.
"That was fun!" says Minnie.

Suddenly, Butch and Bella run past, pulling Goofy behind them.

"Slow down, doggies!" yells Goofy. **"Whoa!"**

"We've got to help Goofy, fast!" says Mickey. **"Oh, Toodles!"**

Mickey picks the Mystery Mouseketool. It's a big sock!
"Come here, doggies!" shouts Mickey.
"Look what I have for you."
  The dogs stop running and play with the sock.

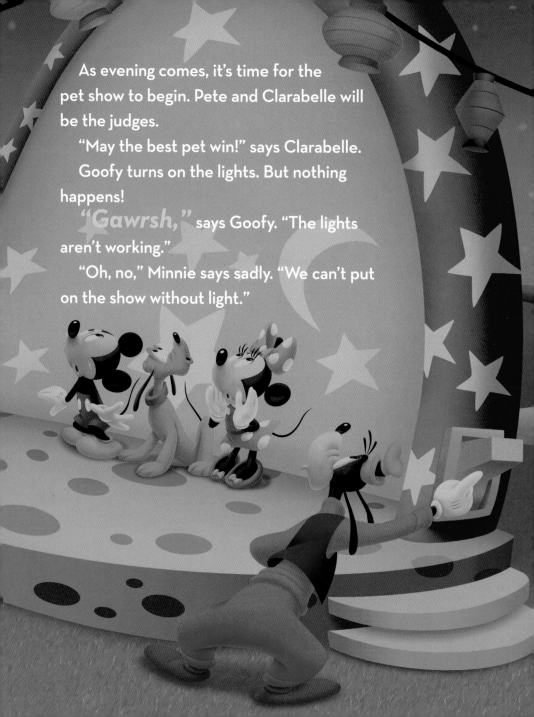

As evening comes, it's time for the pet show to begin. Pete and Clarabelle will be the judges.

"May the best pet win!" says Clarabelle.

Goofy turns on the lights. But nothing happens!

"Gawrsh," says Goofy. "The lights aren't working."

"Oh, no," Minnie says sadly. "We can't put on the show without light."

Mickey knows just what to do.

"Oh, Toodles!" he calls once more. Toodles rushes to the stage. He has one more Mouseketool—a jar full of fireflies!

"Can the fireflies light up the paper lanterns?" asks Mickey. Pluto barks and wags his tail.

"You betcha, Pluto," says Mickey. **"Super cheers!"**

The colorful lights are beautiful.
"Now it's time for Pluto's All-Star Pet Show!" Mickey calls.
"Woof-woof," barks Pluto.

Donald brings Boo-Boo Chicken to the stage. He does a
chicken dance!
Wonderful!

Next Butch and Bella twirl and prance in costumes.
Delightful!

Minnie and Goofy hold up hoops as Figaro and Mr. Pettibone
do tricks.
Amazing!

Captain Jumps-a-Lot and Fiona dazzle the audience with their jumping trick. **Fantastic!**

Clarabelle and Pete can't decide which pet should win
Best in Show. They ask Minnie for help.
"All our pets are the best," says Minnie with a smile.
"So they all win!"